# SEA GIFTS

# SEA GIFTS

by
## GEORGE SHANNON

illustrated by
## Mary Azarian

David R. Godine · Publisher
Boston

First published in 1989 by
David R. Godine, Publisher, Inc.
Post Office Box 450
Jaffrey, New Hampshire 03452
*www.godine.com*

Library of Congress Cataloging-in-Publication Data
Shannon, George.
Sea gifts.
Summary: A man who lives simply by the sea explores
the shore each day for treasures such as a glass bubble from
a fishing net, an empty shell, or wood to warm his home.
1. Children's poetry, American. [1. Seashore—Poetry.
2. American poetry.] I. Azarian, Mary, ill. II. Title.
PS3569.H335S43   1989   811'.54   88-45429
ISBN 1-56792-109-4

*First softcover printing*
Printed in the United States of America

*Both from and to*
Jerry Granger & Goldie Rosenzweig

Tucked like a secret
between the sea and cedar woods
sits the home hand-built
by the man who trades with the sea.

With coffee as the sun comes up
he pulls on boots and walks the shore
carefully stepping from stone to stone.
Cautious of seaweed growing wet from rocks
and anemones hiding in puddles of sea.

Step after step his eyes read the rocks,
searching for treasures high tide
left behind.

One day it's a handle of white and deep red
cracked free from its purpose,
just right to add to the rest
on his wall.

Another day roots grown into a fist
holding a favored rock inside.
And once, a blue glass bubble
from a fishing net
lost long ago on the world's other side.

As he gathers each gift he holds it high,
wondering the story it holds inside
of where and how and when it was.
Of those it left
and why.

Of an empty shell
he wonders how any could leave
such a handsome home.
And quietly says,
"Come join the village
on my shelf."

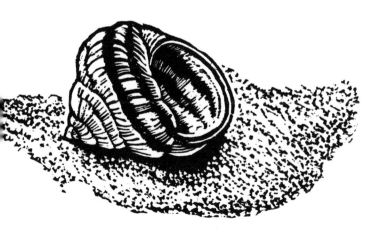

On he walks with welcome smiles
for other gifts
that are best never held.

Beds of sunfish—
all soft shiny blooms
of spring flower jam.

And some days a wish
on a blue starfish
that shines like the night.

Each day each walk
the shore is new
the sea is fresh,
its pattern of ripples telling the weather
and how many jackets the man will wear
as he gathers gift wood.

The largest,
whole trees storm-pulled from shores,
he ties to boulders
till friends can help.

Wood broken from boats
and packing crates
he saves to mend his home
that he keeps warm
with the smaller logs
he saws and chops.

Then splits to stack.

All ready to deny the cold.

Those pocket size or near enough
he borrows for his evening joy.

When home and warm, with all chores done
he watches the sea ease silver to black.

Then lights the lamp.

Pulls out the wood.

His windows on the sea
now mirrors.

Silent and still
he studies each piece,
looking to see what waits
to be freed.
Then opens his knife
and begins to cut.

His tongue shifting left
then right.
Left again
as the knife blade turns.

With every few cuts
he stops to look,
dusting slivers on the cat below.
Looking and carving.

Turning and carving
sliver by chip
he works for hours
till he says

"There."
And a frog is born.
A raven's wing
or a leaping fish.
Each as different
as the wood he finds.

Each made for the making
and made for trade.
Gift for gift upon the rocks.

And with coffee as the sun comes up
he pulls on boots
and walks the shore
leaving his work
for the high tide's hands.

Walks on finding treasures.

More sea gifts
for the sea itself.